The Courtship of the Glen

~~ The Glen Highland Romance ~~
Colin and Caitir's Story
by
Michelle Deerwester-Dalrymple

Table of Contents

If you love this book, be sure to **leave a review!** Reviews are life blood for authors, and I appreciate every review I receive!

Love what you read? Want more from Michelle? **Click the image below to receive Gavin's story,** *The Heartbreak of the Glen,* the free Glen Highland Romance short ebook, free books, updates, and more in your email inbox

<u>Get your free copy by signing up here!</u>[1]

[2]

---

1. https://view.flodesk.com/pages/5f74c62a924e5bf828c9e0f3

2. https://view.flodesk.com/pages/5f74c62a924e5bf828c9e0f3

Chapter One: A Chance Meeting

"**W**here are ye? I'll find ye, for certain," Colin whispered more to himself than anyone near him.

Apple-green light filtered through a small copse of trees as Colin MacLeod stepped on quiet toes after the rabbit that had scuttled into the bushes. If he made any sound, he'd be discovered for certain.

The glen behind him swept out through a heavy moorland and up the small foothills where the seat of Clan MacLeod, and his home, nestled against the rock nearly to the snow that still enclosed the higher mountains. Thistle, bluebells, and moss populated the glen with hues of blues and purples against the green and white moor, and the sound of trickling water at a nearby melting creek made the glen second only to Heaven.

No wonder the Highlands were the most prized land in all the world.

The beauty of the glen was lost on the young man as he picked his way over the rock, flowers, and grass, his hazel-green eyes scanning the scrub in front of him. He stopped moving forward, using his ears where his eyes failed him, listening for any scuttling that would tell him where the rabbit hid.

His brothers were far enough away not to disturb his hunt, and for that he was grateful. His younger brothers, while they needed to learn to hunt, were often more of an encumbrance than a help when Colin hunted — in which he meant they were loud.

Colin, however, had honed his skills with his father's tacksman and hunter, Fingall MacLeod. But as the man aged, his brothers were not recipients of the man's knowledge. As the eldest of the MacLeod sons, it fell to Colin to train his brothers when his father was not able.

Something scuttled, and Colin whipped around, his bow at the ready.

His brothers could be tiring though, especially when Colin wanted to actually hunt something. More often than not, his brothers chased away any game, and they came home empty-handed, and Colin was craving rabbit for supper and did not want to wait for the Whitsunday celebratory feast.

Mistress Annys, the chatelaine, told him if he could bring one home, she would serve rabbit stew for the evening meal. She did not have to ask Colin twice. He grabbed his bow and his worn, leather quiver, abandoned his brothers, and set out to find the closest warren.

Spring was becoming well-entrenched, so finding a nice, plump one would not be too difficult.

A rustling in the brush where the throng of bare trees ended alerted him his prey was at hand.

"There ye are," he said in a hushed tone.

Keeping one eye on the brush and focusing his aim to the ground, he moved forward silently to the edge of the flora, his arrow pulled taut.

He stepped through the tree line, expecting the see a fat rabbit in the crux of the bushes. Instead, he found a young woman, mayhap his age and nearly as tall, clutching *his* dinner to her burgeoning chest.

Her impossibly black, blacker than night, hair hung around her shoulders, a wisp of it pulled away from her face that was as white as fresh milk and served as a perfect frame for the most brilliant blue eyes he had ever seen.

Frozen in place, Colin dropped his bow to his side, his gaze never leaving the woman. She as well didn't move, staring right back at him. They stood that way for several heartbeats until the rabbit wiggled in her arms and the startling beauty ran off across the shadowy valley on the far side of his father's land.

Shaking his head to regain his senses, Colin chased after her.

SHE WAS FAST, SHOCKINGLY fast for a girl in leather, slipper-like shoes. She slipped in and around the rocks and bushes, over damp clumps of earth. Colin, for all he was a well-built young man, able to keep pace with the older men of the clan wearing a dirk and a broadsword and ride like he was one with the horse, the lass could run over the moorland faster than he could. Not only did she steal his dinner, she also ran faster than he did. If he wasn't so inflamed by her beauty, his ire would be.

His mind raced with his feet — *how dare this woman steal his meal? Look him in the eye? Not recognize him? The audacity!*

Colin was not known for his modesty. Hot-headed is what his father oft called him.

A small cottage rose from the edge of the bushes, and he watched as the girl rushed past several chickens, leaving them squawking in the muck, and push through the doorway. She thought she had eluded him, Colin chuckled to himself. As the son of the chieftain, he felt he was an intimidating figure at the doorstep. Puffing his chest out and stretching to his full height, he rapped against the splintering wooden door and called out to the occupants, the young woman in particular.

"Open in the name of your Laird. I am Colin MacLeod, son of Laird Alpin MacLeod, and I demand entrance. And the return of my supper!"

The door creaked open a crack, and a cloth-wrapped elderly woman peered out.

"What's ye say? The Laird, he's 'ere?" the woman croaked.

The old woman was not the woman he expected. Was the lass hiding within?

"Nay, woman. 'Tis his son, Colin MacLeod. I demand entrance."

There, he established his authority and now the door should open —

But mid-thought, the heavy wood door slammed closed. Colin stood with his nose at the wood, staring stupidly.

"Um, 'ello?" he tried again. The door remained secured, even as he rattled at the handle. They bolted it from the inside.

He would see about that. 'Twas early, and the weather was mild and fair. Colin sat his trews on the rickety bench by the door, deciding to bide his time. The old woman and the striking girl would not get the best of Colin.

The afternoon passed with relative boredom. Colin drew in the dirt with a stick, tossed pebbles as far into the grasses as he could, and created dreamy conversations that he would have with the women once he gained access. His stomach rumbled as he reflected on the loss of his supper.

He barely noticed how low in the sky the pale sun had traversed until the door opened. Jumping up and wiping his hands on his tunic, he pulled himself up to his full height, ready for a confrontation with the old woman again.

Only this time, the young woman stood there, looking down her nose at him as if he were nothing more than mud on her slipper.

"ARE YE STILL HERE?" she finally spoke.

Colin's mouth fell open, gaping like a fish freshly yanked from a loch. Her voice was like the water that trickled over the mossy stones of an inlet, clean and crisp. A swipe of ash marred her cheek, but somehow the smudge only highlighted her beauty. She was every beautiful piece of the world in human form. Her shift pulled tight against her breasts as she wiped her surprisingly dainty hands on a scrap of cloth hanging from her skirts.

"Can ye no' speak?" Her eyes squinted as she inquired.

Colin snapped his mouth shut, his teeth knocking together painfully.

"Nay, nay, I can. I can speak," he sputtered out.

"Och, ye have a stutter then!" she exclaimed.

"What? Nay, I dinna stutter!" he protested. *Why could he no' string a thought together?*

Her smooth raven eyebrows knitted together. "Then what is wrong with ye, lad? What do ye want here?"

Lad? This young woman was calling him a lad? "Who are ye calling lad?" Colin's voice rose to a pitch, and the young lass barked out a laugh.

"Is there nay anyone else about?" She whipped her hand around, indicating the shallow valley, empty but for the two of them and some birds flitting in the brush.

Never had the Laird's son been rendered so speechless. She confounded him all the more.

"I am nay a lad," he started, the need to exert his authority rising heartily. He must salvage some pride. "Do ye ken who I am?"

Perchance the lassie was simple-minded, though Colin could not suppose that to be true, given how well she mystified him. Perchance she honestly didn't know her chieftain's family?

"Should I?" she appeared non-plussed.

"Weel, aye. Ye should. I am Colin Alpin MacGregor MacLeod, son of Laird Alpin MacLeod."

The ebony-haired lass remained silent, as though she expected something more.

"Did ye hear me?" he asked.

"Aye."

Colin rubbed his hand across his chin, scratching at his patchy, recently grown beard.

"Have ye no' respect for your Laird or his son?"

"Why should I?"

He blinked several times at her answer. Was she discourteous? Or simply uncouth? Had she no respect for her betters?

"Because I am the son of your chieftain!" Colin exploded.

"Nay, ye are naught to me. Ye chase my rabbit, try to bang down my door, and speak rudely to me. Ye are no' deserving of respect from me."

Colin MacLeod's jaw fell impossibly lower.

"Your rabbit? I was hunting that rabbit! 'Tis to be my supper!"

Colin lurched forward as though rushing the doorway to find said rabbit of dispute. The dark-haired lass screeched and leapt at the door, blocking his passage.

"Dinna get my rabbit! 'Tis my supper. Get your own!"

Colin stood dumbfounded. Not only did the lass speak so disrespectfully, she was physically blocking him, holding up a milky white hand against his tunic. Her touch halted him completely. His chest heaved and shook at the feel of her hand on his body, her warmth bleeding through, and his mind swam in a confusing blend of thoughts and desires. He had a sudden urge to lean forward and kiss the perplexing lass on her reddened lips.

Rubbing his hand over his face again to dispel the conflicting thoughts, Colin made to speak again, opening his mouth, only to watch the lass swirl about in her tattered skirts and slam the door closed.

Chapter Two: Inner Conflict

THE DUST OF THE DOOR lightly coated his rusty brown hair and scraggly beard. He tried pounding on the door again, but silence was the sole response. Growling in anger, he stormed off the way he had come, through the slender copse of trees and their long green-hued shadows toward home.

Ire and frustration at the audacity of the lass battled with a strange, raging desire that flowered in his chest and loins. These notions made him feel dizzy. How could he experience such anger and longing at the same time?

Having an empty stomach made the indignation worse. As he burst into the kitchens, he yelled to Mistress Annys to forget any rabbit stew this day. Colin swooped up the stairwell toward his chambers to retrieve his sword. He needed to take out his anger on someone, and the wooden stump in the yard would encounter a severe beating his day. But that wouldn't be good enough, he knew.

"Josiah!" he bellowed as he grabbed his scabbard from its hanging place at the hearth. "Josiah! Get your sword and meet me in the yard!"

Josiah MacLeod, Colin's childhood friend, had spent the past three years training at the house of a MacKenzie laird, and the young man's skills were unmatched, except by Colin himself. When it came time to relieve frustrations, Colin wanted no other opponent facing him.

Garbed in a leather hauberk and a grimace, Colin stomped to the yard with all the frustration and ire of an affronted young man. His body was hale, but his pride was horribly shattered. 'Twas not in his character to hit a woman, no matter how irksome the lass may be, but his blood pumped through his veins with fire. He hoped Josiah was ready to receive his wrath.

Josiah stepped in the yard not long after Colin arrived. With impatient scowls, Colin continued his stomping as he waited for his friend, and his dramatic histrionics attracted the attentions of several other young men working in the stables. They raced to form a loose circle of spectators alternating cheering on the Laird's son and the accomplished squire.

Colin stormed in the dirt, thrusting his sword into the air, loosening his muscles and warming his sword arm. Up, down, thrust. Up, down, thrust. His plaid flapped about his waist, his strong legs moving easily with the weight of the hauberk and commanding sword. 'Twould appear to be a lonely dance if 'tweren't for the dust he kicked up in the warm, dusky sunset. His dark brown hair, damp with sweat, began to cling to his neck, but he never wavered in his movements.

A scratching sound from the side of the yard announced the appearance of the renowned man, Josiah, and his own heavy sword. Instead of showing off as Colin did, the whiskey-haired lad stepped with a cocky, meticulous gait and dragged the tip of his sword on the ground behind him, marking his journey from the MacLeod tower hall to the inner bailey. Unlike Colin, his moves were calm and measured, his bright green eyes fixed on the overwrought Laird's son. His confidence high, Josiah felt assured that Colin's anger would impede his fighting skills, and Josiah would win the day.

Poor Colin, Josiah thought. *'Twould just anger him more*. Josiah briefly considered throwing the battle to grant his Laird's son some solace, but Josiah had never backed down from a challenge. He preferred to keep his reputation intact and teach the hot-headed Colin a lesson. The Laird's son would just have to stew in the loss that was to come.

Once Josiah was at the center of the crowd, he raised his sword to his shoulder and threw a wry grin Colin's way.

"Are ye ready, laddie? Josiah's here to teach ye a lesson!"

His overconfidence sent Colin into a fit. Colin launched himself at Josiah, hacking at the other man's sword with blind fury.

Josiah smiled at Colin's futile sparring. While the Laird's son had skill, of that Josiah had no doubt, and was brawny enough to triumph in any fist fight, the lad had much to learn about control when it came to swordplay.

Sweat pasted Colin's hair to his forehead, and after several short, ineffectual thrusts, and one attempt at an overhead swing, Josiah could see Colin was tiring. The lad put too much effort in parries and thrusts that would have no benefit. He needed to learn when to put his whole weight into a movement, and when to shift lightly and evaluate his opponent.

Josiah pressed his advantage when Colin pulled back to pant at his exertions, bringing his own broadsword down in a fierce attack that took Colin by surprise. The shock on his face was obvious as he attempted to flee from the oncoming steel that glinted in the final rays of the sun. The tip of the sword caught Colin's hauberk, renting it with a long gash.

Colin stilled, watching as Josiah paced around him, a smug look plastered across his hard features. Anger flooded Colin all the more. Taking advantage of Josiah's moment of reprieve, Colin lunged forward, clashing his sword with Josiah's. He followed this move with an aggressive full body attack, slamming his broad shoulders into Josiah's unprepared frame.

Josiah stumbled back, his sword protecting his chest as he caught himself with his left foot. Colin didn't allow his friend to collect himself and instead slammed into him again. Josiah spilled onto the dirt in a full sprawl. He retained his sword until Colin kicked it out of his hand.

"Get up!" Colin commanded, throwing his own sword to the side.

Josiah did as Colin bid, bracing for Colin's next move. The Laird's son did not disappoint. Before Josiah was fully erect, Colin lowered his shoulder and slammed into Josiah's midsection. Emitting a low "oof," his breath left him. Josiah tried to grapple with the larger lad, inserting his arms between Colin and his own body to thrust him away, and Colin tackled him to the ground again. Colin straddled him, ready to pummel his friend while he had the upper hand, when a stern voice carried over the din of the fight.

"Colin MacLeod!" Alpin MacLeod called to his son.

His powerful voice demanded attention, and Colin pursed his lips before rising off Josiah. He reached out his hand to his friend, and Josiah grabbed it, letting Colin help him to his feet before they faced the Laird.

The MacLeod flicked his steel gaze from one young man to the next. His own frustration matched Colin's — he had to leave a meeting with his tacksman to attend his errant son. Would the lad never learn to temper his anger? Alpin shook his head disapprovingly.

"Josiah, does your family ken where ye are?"

Josiah kept his eyes on the ground, too embarrassed to look at his Laird in the eye. "Nay, my Laird," he answered in a sheepish tone.

"Then I expect ye to return to your chores 'afore ye are missed?"

Josiah knew a pass when he saw one and did not hesitate. He lifted his sword off the ground and ran off in a cloud of dust, leaving Colin to deal with his father's anger on his own. Alpin directed his irritated glare at his eldest son.

His greatest pride, tall, brawny Colin, was also Alpin's greatest concern. The lad had grown into a fine young man, for the most part, smart at his numbers, patient with his family, strong in body. But his temper . . . Colin was gaining a reputation for flying into a fury at the least slight. Alpin had done everything in his power to teach his son temperance: lashings, mucking the stable, even taking on women's work in the kitchens, but to no avail.

The lad seemed unteachable when it came to his anger. And Alpin feared what an angry Laird his eldest son would make. What manner of man would Alpin be leaving his clan to when he passed into heaven?

Alpin shook his head again, only this time it was for his son's view alone. The rest of the lads had scattered with Josiah when the Laird appeared, and now 'twas Colin and his father in the darkened yard. Dread filled Colin like ale in a short cup.

WHAT ALPIN WANTED TO do was bend his twenty-year-old son over the fence there in the yard, yank his braes to his knees, and beat his backside until the lad cried like a bairn. But the lad was full grown, and even if that had been an option in the past several years, Alpin doubted its effect this fine spring evening.

Colin, to his credit, had not moved or spoke since his father called to him. He remained rooted to his spot. With his head lowered in deference to his father, Colin was the same height as he was, too big to tan his backside, Alpin knew. The lad was spoiled — what son of the Laird would nay be? But temperance, that had to be taught. Alpin sighed at the largess of the task.

"What brought ye to the yard to challenge Josiah, laddie?" Alpin queried in a low voice.

His father's question was unexpected. Colin was certain the older man would have taken a switch to him at the very least. To question his motives, though? Colin took a moment to collect his wits 'afore replying. How could he explain that an irascible lass with raven tresses had put him in his place, and he did nay ken how to deal with such a treatment? 'Twas embarrassing, to be sure, and he feared admitting such to his father. Indeed, what choice did he have?

"A lass —" he began, then words failed him.

Alpin worked to halt the grin that pulled at his face. So, his son was flustered over a lass? He raised one inquisitive eyebrow. 'Twas always the lassies.

"And?" Alpin kept his voice stern. While he may have found his son's motive humorous, Alpin could not make his son aware of that. He crossed his arms to present a falsely menacing front.

"Da!" Colin finally lifted his startling hazel-green eyes to his father. "I dinna ken what to do! She stole my supper, then did no' acknowledge the respect due me as the Laird's son! She slammed her door in my face!"

And at that, Alpin lost control. He threw his head back, laughing loudly and harshly at his son's disconcerting perspective to the point his belly ached. The poor laddie had much to learn of women.

Colin's jaw hung agape at his father's response. He was laughing at him? At the disrespect of this lass? Was his father sick in the head?

"Da!" Colin whined again, and his father waved his hand to silence the lad.

"Och, son," he panted as he tamped down the lingering laughter. He placed a large hand on his son's sweaty head, clasping the lad close. So much to learn. "Come walk with your father and tell me all that transpired today. I think I need to tell ye some secrets regarding women."

"Da, I've had women 'afore. I ken what to do —" Colin tried to defend his sexual prowess, which only caused his father to smirk more.

"Nay son. What ye do betwixt the covers, and what ye need to ken about women are verra different."

Alpin dragged Colin to the edge of the yard by his neck, listening to his son list the great offenses he incurred, before explaining the mysterious nature of women to his forlorn progeny.

WHILE YOUNG COLIN APPRECIATED the heart to heart with his sage father, the fact he was now mucking out the stables *again* left a sour taste in his mouth, not to mention a rotten odor in his nose.

His father did a fair job of not suggesting that Colin was agog over the strange lass from the forest, or that most women wouldn't fawn over him for his titles alone. But the idea that his loins surged for the odd lass horrified Colin. A woman who stole his supper and insulted him? In what realm would he ever find such a woman to his liking?

Colin stabbed angrily at the pile of animal refuse, taking his frustrations out on his irksome chore in the dim barn. He didn't do anything wrong. Josiah kenned the rules of fighting, and resorting to fists if swords were lost was not inappropriate. While Josiah may be the superior swordsman, what good was he as a Highlander if he could not keep his feet whilst using his fists? Colin shook his head at the injustice of it all.

Once finished, he returned to the keep, hoping to have a housemaid aid him with his stained and smelly plaid and tunic. Perchance the lass he found could help him with more than just cleaning his clothing. His handsome face beamed at the prospect, only to waver when the seductive image that danced in his head was of a lass with raven locks and sparkling blue eyes.

Dropping his red and black plaid in the basket for the housemaid, he sat on the stool by his bedding, letting that same dark-haired maiden dance in his head all the more. His body reacted unbidden, his cock flexing as he imagined himself undressing the lass, pulling the saffron colored kirtle from her high, full breasts. Allowing his mind to revel in the fantasy, he placed his hand on his shaft, working it at a steady pace until his ballocks flexed and his excitement clenched deep in his body. Colin reached the point of no return, his hand working industriously to bring his climax.

The entire time, the dark-haired lass frolicked before his closed eyes.

Chapter Three: Sage Advice

"GRANDMOTHER," THE LASS called out to the old woman resting on a roped chair near the hearth. The air outside was unseasonably warm, spring being kind this year, so the fire burned low — just enough to keep the hanging pot bubbling.

The rabbit provided enough stew to last several days, and every time Caitir ate, she relished in the taste made sweeter by the fact she had obtained it from the pompous laddie. In fact, she found herself thinking of the handsome but obtuse young man too often, giggling under her breath at the memory of his discomfited look as she closed the door on his face.

Her grandmother noted the lass's lighter disposition and commented on it as they supped.

"Caitir," her aged voice was little more than a croak. "What have ye been thinking about since the laddie appeared these days past?"

A deep flush colored Caitir's milky white skin a lovely rose. While her grandmother had never addressed her beauty, believing the old adage that beauty is only on the skin and that age comes to all, many in the marketplace had remarked on her stunning looks. Across from her grandmother at the table, Caitir's looks were only accentuated by the blush. A rush of pride preceded a streak of fear. The elderly woman kent her time on God's earth was limited, coming to an end soon, but she feared what would become of her stunning granddaughter once she was gone.

The lass could live in this tiny cottage in the woods, but the grandmother did not want her to live alone. Loneliness, the old woman knew, was the only true hell on earth.

And if the Laird's son found an interest in her granddaughter, an interest that may lead to marriage? Even an old woman could dream.

"I dinna ken the lad, grandmother," the lass's voice was curt, trying to hide her emotions, grandmother was certain. A gentle, knowing smile tugged at her deep wrinkles.

"Ye could ken the lad, Caitir," grandmother admonished.

Caitir started to roll her eyes but caught herself so as not to insult the woman who all but raised her. Grandmother taught her respect for those who earned it and deserved her respect more than anyone else she kenned. Caitir remained quiet, slurping at her stew before answering.

"I dinna believe he is the manner of lad I should ken," she admitted to her grandmother. "I dinna care for his demeanor. And he's the Laird's son. Even should I desire such a match, he is surely betrothed to a noblewoman of high birth. His father would no' permit the lad to wed outside his station."

Grandmother rested her wizened face in her hand, gazing at the young beauty on the other side of the worn, pine table. Caitir truly had no notion of just how powerful her attractiveness could be, especially when paired with such a spry disposition. The old woman bowed her head, choosing the most shrewd words she could manage.

"Aye, station does play a role with those who are highborn, but nay always. Sometimes the heart leads, and yon laddie has no' so powerful a family as to be forced into an undesired match. Do ye ken my words?"

Grandmother raised her watery blue gaze to catch her granddaughter's bright one. The lass was nothing if not astute. She kent the meaning in her grandmother's advice.

And while she disagreed, her grandmother's concern regarding a potential husband weighed heavily on her. She must wed soon; she was more than of age. If not the Laird's son, then mayhap another, kinder, less pompous lad from the clan would suit.

Market day was approaching. Perchance she could use the time selling her herbs to find a potential suitor, a chore she dreaded. While finding a husband may ease her grandmother's fretful nature, having the Laird's lad try to command her chapped her skin. She was a free spirit; a Highland wood sprite, and she would nay be tamed.

THE MORNING OF MARKET day was the first morning in days where Mother Nature decided to rescind her fine weather and replace it with damp, weeping rain.

Caitir took extra time packing her herbals in her basket, placing the most susceptible to rain at the bottom of the tightly bound basket. She placed a scrap of wool atop the stack of herbals, tucking the edges in against the sogginess of the day.

Wrapped in her own warm wool, Caitir stepped onto the sodden pathway and picked her way along the muddy trail to the market. Her heart sunk the more she walked, sensing the trip would be a worthless endeavor. The Scots were hardy people, but sales of herbals were always low when the rain encroached on the market.

Steeling her resolve, and deciding to make the most of the day, Caitir ducked under the covering of her narrow booth squeezed between two smiths and pulled the damp wool from her face. With barely enough room to turn around, Caitir displayed her wares, keeping most of the herbals as dry as possible under the thatched cover. Once the delicate stalks bound with wool thread were set on the table, Caitir was ready for inquisitive patrons.

As her grandmother was renowned for her potions and herbs, her healing and blessings, the herbal packets sold with little effort from

Caitir. At most, she answered questions of which was most effective, and after she pointed to the proper packet, the patron would snatch it off the table as if the packet may disappear. Since she had tutored under her grandmother for most of her life, Caitir's own advice was often sought. One of her most popular items was the love token — a ribbon tied around heather and thistle, held above smoked sage and charmed with a love chant. Women, old and young alike, coveted this singular packet and saved their coin to purchase it when Caitir made it available.

That day's early morning was slow, with only two calming draughts sold by mid-morning. And as though God and nature heard her complaints, all the sellers at the market breathed a lively sigh of relief when the pasty sun finally parted the dismal clouds, and its weak rays cast a sparkling glow on the wet booths. Caitir's boots, caked with mud, served as a reminder of her trek in the rain. She pushed her woolen wrap off her hair and prepared for buyers.

And she was not wrong. All too soon, more and more open space appeared on her table as the herbal packets sold. Most of the buyers desired healing herbs, ones that mixed with warm water or ale and provided relief for a cough or a fever, typical for early spring when many were still trying to recover from winter ills. A few buyers, though, inquired for other potions — ones for love, to quicken with a child, to help elderly kin move more easily. Caitir passed the packets to the patrons with a smile on her face and a recommendation for usage.

Her buyers kept her busy enough that she didn't see the young men approaching her booth.

Chapter Four:
Temperaments

Colin, with Josiah and several other young men from the keep, waited for the rain to abate before venturing to the market. Rarely did they purchase any items, rather they spent the time admiring girls and searching for perfect weapons. Dirks that could be easily tucked into a legging or sporran were especially desired.

Those and foodstuffs. Several of the booths offered specialty foods Mistress Annys did not prepare for those of the keep. Dried lamprey and pickled herring, stinking snacks craved by Colin and his young kinsmen, disappeared quickly when they came to market.

Colin also noted several young men from the MacKenzie clan came to market day, as many from the western side of the MacKenzie clan lands did. 'Twas a shorter walk than hiking over craggy swells to the MacKenzie market. The MacLeod's were amicable and kenned most of the men in the clan, but one young man in particular, Broccin MacKenzie, raised Colin's ire. The lad once tried to best Colin in a fist fight, and before Colin reigned as the victor, they were pulled apart and admonished in plain view of their kinsmen. The MacLeod lad had not forgotten and, against Josiah's more sage advice, vowed to get the best of Broccin.

And out of the corner of his eye, Colin saw that very opportunity unfold before him.

Clutching a slippery pickled herring in his thick grip, the pickled juices dripping from his palm, he turned his head to take a large bite when the familiar blue-green of the MacKenzie plaid swayed before him. His eyes tracked up to the man's face, and Colin's jaw remained wide open, herring ignored.

Not only was the cocky MacKenzie lad here in the marketplace, and Colin's father was not, the MacKenzie lad was at the herbal booth, gaping not at the wares on the table, but at the strikingly beautiful, raven-haired woman selling them. 'Twas the very same lass from the woods. The one who thieved his rabbit. The one who insulted him. The one who haunted his dreams.

And Broccin leaned over the table, his gaze dropping to Caitir's breasts rather than her wares. While Caitir tried to keep a reasonable distance, the lad leaned over farther, his face a mere hairs breath from her luscious, smiling lips. Her coloring reminded him of a stained glass he had seen in a kirk once, only more vibrant, more real.

"What are ye sellin' today, lassie?" His fishy breath was hot on her face, and she stepped back from the table. Her slender hand waved over her items.

"I have several calming draughts," she pointed to the woven packets on the table, "but I think ye would be more interested in this, a tonic for young men, to help them smell more appealing." Her suggestion was not lost on the large lad, whose brow furrowed with insult. She smiled at his offended response.

Colin remained stock-still as he watched the scene before him, his herring long forgotten. At first, he feared his chance to win the lass had passed, her smile toward Broccin encouraging him to press his advantage. When the MacKenzie lad reached for her upper arm and pulled her close, Colin noted her expression change, a shadow of unease flitting across her delicate features. Broccin's advances were not as welcome as Colin first believed.

A shockingly familiar, but unwelcome fire built in Colin's belly, fueled by anger and, he hated to admit, jealousy. He didn't understand why he was jealous — all he could think was he wanted that sparkling blue gaze and those enticing lips facing him. Josiah was speaking, commenting on a random booth or another, stopping mid-sentence as Colin thrust his limp herring to his clansman.

Josiah grasped the fish and turned to see what had caught Colin's gaze. His heart fell out of his chest with dismay. *Surely Colin would nay start a fight here, on market day?*

He realized the insanity of his notion as soon as Colin spun on his heel toward the MacKenzie lad at the herbal booth. Of course, Colin would start a fight. Noting the black-haired beauty selling the wares, he understood MacKenzie's interest and the dark pallor of anger that shaded Colin's face. Dropping the fish to the dirt, Josiah rushed after the Laird's son, yanking him back by the collar of his tunic.

"Colin!" Josiah hissed in his ear. "Dinna make a scene here. Do ye ken what your father will do?"

Colin shrugged him off, never breaking his stride. Temperance had never been his strong suit. Broccin only noticed the oncoming brute when he saw Caitir's eyes widen, and not at him. Her gaze passed over his shoulder, and when he turned around, his sights found Colin's enraged face.

BROCCIN HAD NO TIME to move, as Colin shoved the MacKenzie lad away from the table, a low growling emanating from deep in his chest. Skittering backwards, Broccin barely retained his balance before launching a verbal strike at Colin.

"What ails ye, MacLeod?" Broccin hollered hoarsely, attracting attention from kinsmen and women in the marketplace. The din of the market quieted abruptly as patrons eyed the quarrel from under booths and head wraps. A good fight would make for an exciting market day indeed.

Ignoring the stares of the villagers, Colin pressed forward at Broccin. Though the Laird's son stood nearly half a head taller, the MacKenzie lad was thicker, a dense young man, and was at least a stone heavier. And 'twas said that the lad knew how to use that girth, having quite the reputation as a scrapper.

Josiah stepped up behind Colin in a show of support; 'twould nay do to let his Laird's son and closest friend fall victim. But when he felt the heat practically steaming from Colin, he believed that, perchance, his assistance would nay be necessary. He had never seen Colin in such an enraged state. His eyes flicked to the raven-haired lass standing in stunned silence behind her table. *Was this all over a lowly lass?*

"The lady doesna seem to care for your attentions, Broccin. I would suggest ye depart the stalls." Colin's hands formed into fists as he spoke.

"And will ye be the one to make me leave?" Broccin spat as he taunted. 'Twas enough to send Colin over the edge. "What if the lassie wants me to stay?"

"My lady," Colin's attention shifted to Caitir, whose bright blue eyes widened at the address. *She was no lady, to be sure.* Caitir thought. *Why would he address her as such?* "Is this young man o'er stepping his bounds with ye?"

His tone was so different from the manner by which he spoke to her in the wood, refreshingly respectful, and she credited him that. Her pink lip twitched in recognition and appreciation. Mayhap 'twas more to the Laird's son than she thought; mayhap her grandmother was right. *Again.*

"Ooch, only a bit offensive, milord. Nothing I can no' handle."

"Would ye like for me to escort the laddie from your table then?"

Caitir only nodded, that tiny smile peeking from her lips. Colin bowed toward her politely, his full brown hair shining from the damp weather. The gray-blue skies made his eyes appear more green than brown, and for a moment, she was deeply engaged by his appearance and behavior. She caught herself and cleared her throat while Colin returned his attentions to the other lad.

"Weel, MacKenzie, the young lady wants ye gone. Come wi' me or I shall make ye leave."

"Ooch, will ye now?" Broccin puffed up his chest and reared like a steed at Colin.

He knew he could not let Broccin get the upper hand. Though Colin was proud of his own fighting skills, the extra layer of fat on the lad's frame could take him down, and the MacKenzie lad was no lax fighter. When Broccin attempted a roundhouse punch, Colin knew enough to weave beyond his reach, then swing his own fist upward at Broccin's jaw.

The punch didn't land as solidly as Colin would have liked, and Broccin managed to bring his hammer fist up and catch Colin in the nose as he reared back. Colin shoved at Broccin, snapping a weak punch on the side of the lad's head. Another awkward hit, but the damage was done. Broccin stumbled backwards, slipping in the mud. Colin caught his arm and hoisted him upright.

"Dinna try that again, laddie. 'Tis time for ye to leave."

Colin tipped his head to Josiah to follow him, as the rest of the MacKenzie lads fell in line behind Broccin. Colin led the coterie past the rectory to the crossroads that would lead the MacKenzies back to their own clan lands.

Once the lads were on their way in the unending drizzle, Josiah patted Colin on the back.

"Colin! Ye surprise me! I would have thought ye would end up tussling with the ogre in the mud. Yet here ye are, with naught but a smather of blood on your nose. I would almost say I am proud of your restraint. Could yon black-haired lassie be the reason?"

Colin shoved his friend to the side, but the flicker of humor in his eyes granted Josiah leave for a full laugh. Ignoring the taunts, Colin worked his way through the muck to Caitir's stall. The gawking of the locals had ended, now that the fight was over, and the only eyes that were on him belonged to the young woman he sought.

"Ooch, milord. Your nose!" Caitir grasped a thin cloth, and pouring a splash of a cloudy liquid over it, she handed it to him. She gestured that he place it under his bleeding nose.

"'Twill help stop some of the bleeding until yet can get ye home. Then place the coldest water ye can find upon a cloth and press it against your face. 'Twill help the swellin' as well."

Colin accepted the scrap of fabric, letting his fingertips linger over hers as he took it from her hand. A rush of pink stained her cheeks, and Colin dropped his eyes, suddenly very interested in the cloth.

"Thank ye," she said in a low voice.

In the strange way the world seemed to work, they both noted that their understanding of one another had shifted, throwing them together like oats in a bin, and Caitrin pondered what it meant.

"Ye are welcome," he responded, and the air between them became hot and awkward. "I should return home. Take care o'my nose, as ye suggested."

This time when he spoke, his hazel gaze caught her blue one and refused to let go. Her own gaze fueled a fire deep within him, one distinctively dissimilar from the heat of his anger. And as much as he didn't want to leave, he could fathom no shameless reason to stay. Gawking at a pretty lass was a shameless reason.

"Aye, and here." She handed him yet another item, a small cloth packet emitting a pungent odor. "Mix it with warm water or mead and drink it up. 'Twill help any pain that remains."

Colin nodded and began to walk off. Caitir noted he couldn't stop looking back over his shoulder at her as he departed.

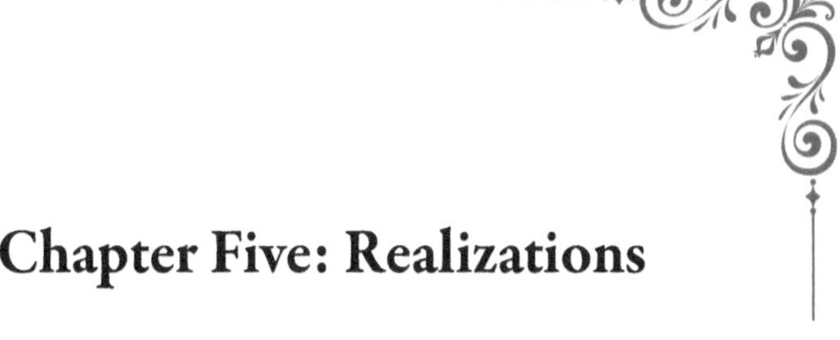

Chapter Five: Realizations

Mistress Annys fretted and bustled about the kitchens to nurse Colin's battered nose. She noted it didn't appear broken (he could have told her that — a broken nose would have sent him to his knees in a frenzy of pain, he was certain), but bruising had spread across his face up to his eye, and it looked so much worse than it truly was. Still, the attentions were welcome. 'Twas nice to be babied sometimes, Colin admitted to himself.

He retired to his room to shed his muddy stockings and dry his tartan. He was closing the door to his chamber just as his father entered the narrow stone hallway. The man's always stoic expression gave Colin pause. *What did he do this time? Did his father know about his scuffle with Broccin?*

"Your uncle Hamish was in the village this morning and told me you were involved in a skarmash."

So he did know. "Da, 'twasn't like that a'tall," Colin began, but his father waved him off.

"Dinna interrupt your elders." His strong voice demanded obedience. "But from what he told me, ye managed, for the first time in all your hot-headed life, not to succumb to your baser natures. That ye did take a hit to the face —" Here his father inclined his head at Colin's bruising. Colin placed a subconscious hand on his face. "But ye worked to subdue the MacKenzie attacker, and ye did so in defense of a bonny lass who found herself at his mercy. Is what your uncle told me true?"

Colin hung his head, so he missed the amusement dancing behind his father's eyes. Little did he know his father had been waiting, and not patiently, for the lad to exhibit some measure of man who would show his abilities as a Laird. Finally, *finally*, the older man had evidence of his son's potential. And while the lad still resorted to violence, 'twas the sort of violence that made a Highland warrior. And for a lass? Well, Alpin could nay ignore the implications of *that*.

"Lad, I am verra proud. Ye needed to learn to use your position and power to serve your clan, nay dictate it. And to temper that power. Ye accomplished that this morning. Come wi' me to my study. Let us see what else ye can do for the clan."

Colin's head snapped up to peer at his father, his confidence in himself regarding his father's opinion rose as the sun on a bright morning. For all his score of years, he felt like a bairn in the presence of his father, the chieftain. Today, his father regarded him as a man. Grinning, he trailed after his father as they walked toward the study.

THE JOURNEY BACK TO her cozy cottage passed without notice, as Caitir's thoughts drifted elsewhere. Specifically, to the tall, handsome son of the Laird.

His respectful demeanor toward her, removing the smelly MacKenzie man, allowing her to tend his poor nose, was so different from the spoiled laddie she had met in the woods. Her mind reveled in recalling the images of the Laird's son, his plaid tossed over his shoulder, and how he moved with confidence against the heavier youth. Her grandmother's words echoed in her head, that she could come to know Colin, and her heart leapt with hope, perchance, she would see the man again soon.

Caitir was already planning another venture into the copse of trees near the glen, by the chieftain's keep, in an effort to see him, while at the same time scolding herself for having such scandalous thoughts. But why did her mind spin and her breath catch whenever she recollected the way he looked back over his shoulder at her?

The end of the trail through the sparse scrub announced her arrival at grandmother's house, and though a thin rain had resumed, the damp had not bothered her in the least.

"I would hope such a smile would be for me?"

Though her heart did a quick jump at the words, the thick voice told her at once 'twas nay the voice she desired to hear. Caitir's chest closed with a moue of fear when the sight of the burly MacKenzie man stepped into her view. She flicked her eyes around his broad shoulders, hoping to squeeze past and run for the cottage, but he shifted as if in anticipation of her motives. The moue of fear swelled into her belly.

Surely, the lad knew when he was beat? Surely, he wouldn't try to attack her person? These thoughts fell in a jumble in her mind as he moved closer.

"Aw, now my lovely lass. Ye dinna have a smile for me?"

Trying to hide her fear under her biting tongue, Caitir tossed her mass of full black hair under her wool wrap, her piercing gaze challenging his own.

"Now, ye see here, laddie. I have work to do today, and ye are keeping me from it. Ye had your fun in the village, now run along home."

Her ferocity and condescending tone were not well received. Broccin's dark eyes flashed with anger. Unlike the tempered son of the Laird, this one often let anger get the best of him, and such a man was an uncontrollable danger, to be sure. Caitir gripped her basket in both hands and made to march around him.

Broccin shifted his girth to the side, blocking her. In a mocking gesture, he chucked her under her chin, clucking his tongue.

"Lassie, 'tis no way to be speaking to a man who wants ye so." He flicked his eyes toward the clearing near her home. "Such a lass as ye, I'm sure ye kent the best way to please a man."

Horrified, Caitir clenched her jaw while knocking his smelly hand from her face. Aye, she may live on the outskirts of the clan, but that did nay mean she was a woman of ill-repute!

"Dinna speak to me so disrespectfully. I would finish my journey home. By your leave, move so I may pass. I am no' the woman for ye. Find a wanton at your keep or in the village."

This time he gripped her shoulder, and that swell of fear she tried to hide erupted. Her face burned at the youth's audacity and the ache he caused.

"I said nay. Come with me now. Should no' take that long."

Broccin tried to shove her toward the scrub at the edge of the path. She screamed as he handled her, and so focused as she was on trying to elude him, she wasn't prepared for the smack that skimmed across her cheek.

Pain exploded in her head, rocking her backwards, and she lost her grip on her basket of necessaries. She had been hit 'afore — aye, her grandmother didn't spare the rod when Caitir was a bairn — but to be struck in the face by a man was another matter. And panic rode in on that realization. If he struck her so easily, what else was he apt to do?

The lad was pulling at her kirtle, trying to force her breasts into the open air, when a clanging noise reverberated in her ears, and Broccin fell in an unsightly heap in the wet brush.

A bent form in a worn cloak lifted her face to Caitir.

"Grandmother!"

Caitir had never been so relieved to see the elderly woman. For such a tiny, old crone, her grandmother was still strong enough to carry heavy baskets to and from the moorland. Knocking an errant MacKenzie to the ground was nary a feat for the woman.

Grandmother kicked at the senseless lad and reached her hand out to Caitir.

"Come lassie. Let's get ye inside and tend that mark. Do ye have your basket?"

Caitir moved in a dizzying swoop to retrieve it from the ground, her simples still tucked away for safekeeping. Her grandmother took it from her hand.

"Take my arm, dearie. I will no' have ye stumble as ye walked. A fist to the face can take a lot out of ye."

As her grandmother escorted her home, Caitir understood her time as a lass had ended. Her grandmother would nay be on this mortal earth much longer, and Caitir should be safely wed 'afore then. 'Twas apparent that her safety depended on it.

Chapter Six: A Second Chance for a First Impression

Colin's father did not find Colin's interest in the strange, mystic lassie problematic. Frankly, Alpin was ecstatic his son found a woman who kept him confounded and tempered the fire of youth that burned in his belly. Fighting was necessary, even beneficial, when it served a purpose, but violence for violence's sake did not. *Did we want to be like the wayward English?* Alpin always asked.

Knowing how to fight, to stand up to a challenger, to wield a dirk and a broadsword, aye, these were a part of Highland life. But his father was right — far too often Colin used his fists instead of his head and used them far too hard. He didn't scuffle with his kin; he abused them, and such behavior not becoming of the chieftain to be.

'Twas as if a flame of light brightened in his head, fathoming what he could not see 'afore. He was to serve a greater purpose, and a Laird had to earn his clan's respect. The words of the raven-haired lass replayed in his mind: *Ye are nay deserving of respect from me.*

Perchance no' yet. But his actions in the village, and his much better tempered behavior as of late, those were the right start to earning her respect. With steadfast intentions, Colin decided to show the lass his true worth. He had a larger problem presently, however.

He didn't even know her name.

RESOLVING TO RECTIFY his problem, he walked the same path as he had the fateful day he first encountered her — a dark fairy in a bright wood — and wandered in the fog until he emerged at her cottage. Pulling himself up to his full height, he patted at his trews and his tunic, and ran his fingers through his slightly matted hair. Mayhap he should have put it in a queue.

Questioning himself on her doorstep also made him aware he did no' bring a gift. Wasn't a man supposed to bring a gift when courting a lass?

And was that what he was doing? Courting her? He shook his head. Aye, he had to admit it. He was hoping to court the strange, bonny lass whose name he didn't know. Josiah would say he'd lost his head, but the look on his father's face when Colin left after the noon meal told him that his actions were not all that foolish.

Crouching near the edge of the pathway, he selected several early crocuses and thistle into a paltry offering of flowers. Returning to the door, he took a deep breath and knocked.

Caitir opened the door enough to peek one sky-blue eye out. She reminded him of everything beautiful of spring, and he thrust the flowers at her eye.

"Hello, lassie," he started, finding his voice. "I was wondering if ye would care to invite me inside, so I may converse with ye in the presence of your grandmother."

Oh, he sounded pathetic. He had naught courted 'afore. Is this what one did, in courtship?

Caitir didn't move from her space behind the door and continued to stare. His chest grew heavy with embarrassment. Perchance he read her affections in the village wrong? Perchance she did no' care for him? Or she already had a betrothed?

Suddenly the door moved, opening wider, and Caitir stepped into the opening. His eyes burned as they danced over her — the long wool skirt that scarcely touched her bare feet, the way her lush breasts filled out her kirtle, her shining hair dropping from an earthy kerchief. Once his gaze moved to her face, though, his gamy grin disappeared, replaced by the same hardened look she had seen him wear in the village.

His finger reached for her marked cheek, a stark brackish blue against her milky skin. Anger flared inside him, so hot and explosive he feared speaking.

"Who did this to ye?" His voice came ragged, and in a moment that made his heart clench so forcefully he thought 'twould stop beating, the fiery Caitir dropped her eyes in shame.

"'Tis but naught." She tried to wave it off. But Colin wouldn't be dissuaded.

"Lassie, I would no' have ye abused on your own land," he continued.

"Please, I dinna want to be the cause of any strife."

"Lassie —" *Christ's blood, what was her name?* "I dinna believe the strife is yours. Ye did no' strike yourself?"

Her lips tugged into a slight smile at his words. Then his hand was on her cheek, cupping it, and her hand covered it, holding its warmth to her skin.

"'Tis all over now," she told him, trying to calm his fevered temper.

Her hand on his, her soft words, had the desired effect, and his anger cooled. His chest no longer puffed in rage, and his whole body relaxed. He couldn't sustain his anger when she was near. What sort of spell did she cast on him? How did she temper his fury with one gentle touch? Colin's father complimented him on learning temperance, but truly, 'twas the lass. She calmed him, a soft breeze on a warm night.

"Ye are my kin. I should ken who on my land behaves in such a manner?"

"The one is gone from your land. I dinna think he will return." Caitir's eyes flicked down at the crumpled flowers in Colin's hand. "Are those for me?"

Colin's gaze followed hers. The paltry flowers looked even more pathetic now. Regardless, he held them out to her.

"I will get ye a better gift next time," he promised, then pulled the flowers away from her grasp. "Wait. First ye must answer me something."

Her blue gaze, the one that stilled his heart and his breath until he thought the world would fall away, lifted to meet his eyes.

"What is your name?"

SPRING MEANT BURGEONING flora, melting snow, and the blossoming passion between Caitir and Colin. Though their time together was often short, they caught moments whenever they could — after market day, when Colin traversed the moorland and woods to her door, and most often, to meet without watching eyes in the copse of trees between her croft and the keep.

Alpin turned a blind eye to the lad's indiscretions. 'Twas the first time his son took a serious interest in a lass, more than a one-night bedmate, a lass who helped him grow as a man and kept his temper under lock and key. And while the chieftain would have preferred to make a match with a local clansman's daughter, or with the daughter of another Laird, Caitir was a better fit. Colin had snubbed, insultingly in some cases, those young women. What spell the lassie managed to cast, Alpin could only guess.

In the early evening before market day, they met in the woods again. The warmer, dry weather meant they left their tartans behind as they raced to each other's arms. Their lips met as their bodies crushed together in a flurry of kissing and desire. Colin pressed his advantage as far as she permitted, once even reaching below the bodice of her gown to cup the gentle curve of her breast. Then he had to bite his lip, hard enough to draw blood, and step away. He could nay, would nay, attempt anything more until he was well and truly wed.

Not that she would let him get much further anyway. The raven-haired woman was a force.

Amid the licking and kissing, Colin's arms wrapped so tightly around her waist he feared snapping her in two. And she let his erect manhood, which begged and begged for release, press into her belly without comment.

And just as quickly as they thrust together, he withdrew from her, loosening his grasp. She looked up to his pained face, her black eyebrows questioning slashes across her forehead.

"I canna last much longer," he admitted, a rosy stain rising from the light growth of beard. His beard made him look older than his score of years. But when he blushed, he almost resembled a young lad, squeezing at Caitir's heart, and Caitir pressed her hand against that beloved face.

"Much longer for what?" she asked, bewildered.

"For ye. I want ye, Caitir, more than I have wanted anything in my life. And the more I am with ye, God help me, I just want ye more. I canna get enough of ye. I'm crazed from it. And since I want ye so badly, there is but one solution."

His voice was gruff as he swept both of her hands into his larger ones, clutching them to his chest. She felt the erratic, nervous flutter of his heart under his tunic.

"I want ye to wed me," he told her without hesitation. "I want ye for my wife."

Caitir, for once, was speechless. She had known the Laird's son to be impulsive, acting without thinking as young men often do (at least according to her grandmother), but his wish to wed rose above all that.

"Are ye mad?" She stepped back, trying to put space between them, space between herself and his radical proposal.

"Nay, why?" His earnest voice forced a sharp laugh from Caitir.

"Because your father would nary permit such a match. Surely, the son of the chieftain would already have a powerful match arranged?"

Colin pursed his lips and shook his head. Small hairs caught the last of the setting sun and danced around his face.

"Well, 'tis no' such a problem as ye would suggest," he explained. "My father tried that 'afore, has tried it since I was fourteen. Nary a lass to be found that I wanted to wed, or who wanted to wed me. Few lasses want a hot-headed fool for a husband, ye ken?"

"And what makes ye think *I* want such a man as that for a husband? Why should *I* yoke myself to such a fate?" The mocking tone in her voice was subtle, but noticeable. A slow grin spread across Colin's hairy face.

"Ye see, that's the difference. With ye, I am no' a hot-headed fool. Ye soothe me, make me a better man, a man who could well be a respected laird one day. I canna do this without ye. I dinna *want* to do this without ye. If ye say nay, I will have to walk the earth alone for the rest of my days."

This time she cupped his face with both hands, pulling him close. Though she may not believe she would truly be the wife of the Laird apparent, dreams were always welcome.

"We can no' have that, now can we?" she said before she kissed him fully.

Chapter Seven: Promises

Market day came again, and none too soon for Colin who raced past the gate toward the village, Josiah hot on his heels.

Alpin knew something significant was brewing with his son. The lad had been unnaturally quiet for several days, passing the afternoons with his head far above the clouds, unlike his usual brash self. It didn't take much for Alpin to see his son was in love. With the local healer's daughter, no less.

And while he didn't necessarily want his son to marry a lass rumored to be one step above a witch, what the heart wants, especially with a willful young man, the heart gets. 'Twould disappoint many fathers in the northern Highlands, but his son was smitten. Colin finally spoke with him the night 'afore, declaring his love and intentions to wed, challenging his father to stop him. Ahh, the heat of young love, Alpin thought, recalling his own earlier years of burning youthful indiscretions. He would nay challenge his son's choice, though he certainly may have to defend it.

Colin wanted to share the blessed news with his new wife-to-be, and market day would assuredly be a fine time to do so. And he needed a gift for her, a small token — the merchants should have a trinket or some lace that would suffice, and he could give it to her that day in full sight of clan and kin.

The warm weather brought out said clans and kin from near and far, and the choices for gifts abounded. Josiah hovered, looking over Colin's shoulder, giving unsolicited advice at each merchant. When the elder

Duncan tried pushing a hair ribbon onto Colin, Josiah ushered him away, promising that the lassie would certainly prefer a shiny token as a bridal gift.

"Nay socks?" Colin joked, and Josiah cuffed his friend's head as they walked to the silversmith to inquire about a delicate brooch, perchance one engraved with a thistle.

Their attentions directed toward the sparkling brilliance of the sliver smith, they didn't see several young men of the MacKenzie clan approach from the east and missed the rather unfortunate appearance of Broccin MacKenzie. His pride was injured, sorely in his estimation, and he wanted a measure of revenge. While he earned his defeat at the hands of the MacLeod son, his inability to conquer the black-haired wench — being toppled by her grandmother even! — chapped his pride.

And though none knew that an old woman dropped Broccin like a stone, he knew it, and he wouldn't stand for it. Moving indiscernibly beyond the clusters of shoppers and merchants vying for their necessaries, he came upon the wench while her back was turned.

Broccin had also heard that the Laird's son had found the lass bonny enough to pursue, and the lass received him! Ire burned deep and hot in Broccin's gut. He would teach the lassie a lesson about saying nay to Broccin (*with a shovel*, Broccin griped). He rubbed the back of his bony head in remembrance of the crack to his skull.

Stepping up to the stall, he asked for an herbal packet, and when Caitir turned to answer, the high points of color on her cheeks paled as fear crossed her delicate features. Her beauty disarmed him momentarily, but he shook it off and grasped her arm in his furious hand.

"Release me, ye fiend!" Caitir tried to sound bold, as if Broccin was naught more than irritating vermin. Her insides did nay match her voice. Her chest tightened and her knees quivered. Where was Colin? Could he arrive in time to rescue her from Broccin's advances again? What did the unpleasant MacKenzie man want now?

She swung her arm, trying to dislodge his grip, as her eyes darted about looking for someone, anyone, to intervene. The laddie increased his hold, yanking her forward over her narrow table of herbals.

"I willna let a wee lassie and her old grandmother make a fool of me," he hissed in her face, his breath little improved since their last encounter.

"I told ye, unhand me. Ye overstep your bounds, laddie," she commanded with scorn, hoping her words injured his pride enough for him to take his leave.

"We started something in the woods, ye bitter wench, and if ye will spread your thighs for the lanky son of a nothing chieftain, then ye should have no issue spreading them for me."

Broccin practically dragged her over the table, knocking her packets askew in the dirt. She tried to call out, but he worked his hand over her mouth to gag her. Moving quickly to a narrow space beyond a croft off the main market, Broccin shoved her to the ground. Caitir took the moment to cry out, hoping someone would hear her. She also kicked her leather-clad foot out as hard as she could.

Colin and Josiah had barely caught sight of Broccin grappling with Caitir and pushed past the crowd to race to her aid. Colin's rage burned like a late summer fire, and Josiah feared the man would well and truly lose all control this time. A man did no' place his hands on another man's wife, or the woman who would become his wife. And the last thing the MacLeod clan needed was to make an enemy of the MacKenzie's, if Colin did indeed kill Broccin for this offense.

Just as they rounded the corner of the cottage, Caitir caught Broccin at the apex of his own legs, and they watched the husky lad drop once again like a stone. Her aim was true, and the MacKenzie youth would no' be finding recourse between any lasses' thighs anytime soon.

Broccin's throbbing ballocks were not enough punishment for the lad's audacity to put hands on the woman who would be Colin's wife. Rage filled Colin in a burning rush, overflowing in a ruckus of fists and kicks.

Josiah grappled with Colin, trying to calm him and pull him off the abused MacKenzie lad, but Colin was blinded by his rage. His handsome, refined face was a mask of dangerous fury. Caitir collected her senses, sat up, and brushed the loose dirt from her skirt, taking her time. She then rested a delicate hand on Colin's heated arm. Broccin did threaten her after all. He did deserve some manner of a beating, but he didn't deserve to be beaten to death.

"Colin," her pacifying voice carried over the scuffle on the ground, garnering Colin's attention like a spell cast by a fairy.

His fist paused midair, and as she held his gaze, the red heat that marred his skin abated, cooled, and Colin stepped back onto his heels. Threading her fingers through his, Caitir and her stoic presence immediately calmed him. Colin inhaled deeply, as though trying to breathe her in. As he exhaled, she stepped into his arms, and he rested his head against her cheek.

"I should have taught him a better lesson last time," Colin told her.

"Weel, I dinna think the lad will have it in him to try again," she responded.

"Not with what ye did to his ballocks!" Josiah added, interrupting their intimate moment. His rueful grin swept over the young man on the ground. "I would no' wish that punishment on any man!"

"Then keep your hands off my future wife, and ye willna suffer that indignation!" Colin teased.

"Future wife?" Caitir reeled back, her cerulean eyes full of bewilderment. "Dinna joke, Colin. Nay about something so serious."

"'Tis no joke," Colin's tone dropped. "My father is in agreement that I am a better man with ye. He sees that I could be a strong Laird with ye by my side. In fact, I bought this for ye today."

He reached into his lightly stained sporran and retrieved a round silver token. Colin placed it in her palm, and she peered at the trinket, tracing the fine etching with a dainty fingertip.

"What is this?" she asked, lifting that mesmerizing gaze to his eager face.

"A gift." His voice behind his scruffy beard was soft, the rage from minutes before gone. "A bridal gift."

"Nay," her voice shook as she thrust the brooch back at him.

Josiah noted the shift in her tone and eyed this situation, nosy about the outcome of his friend's proposal. So far 'twas not going well.

"What do ye mean, nay? Ye dinna want to wed me?"

Colin's hurt came through in his words and his face. He could not imagine his life without this striking lass who tempered his brashness. Why did she deny him? Panic arrived on the heels of his pain.

"Ooch, I want to wed ye," she explained. "That is true, but I canna wed ye! I am an orphaned lass living on the edge of the clan, born into a tenant family. Some even rumor that I'm a witch! I hear the rumors. I canna believe your father, or the clan, would accept me as your wife."

"Ye are wrong on several counts." Colin clasped her hands as he spoke, ready to defend his decision. "First, my father has approved it. He sees how ye temper my, uh, more irrational tendencies." Caitir raised one slender, dark eyebrow at his choice of words. He ignored it and continued. "And as for the clan, they do no' ken ye the way I do. If I can love ye, they will learn to do the same."

He loved her? Her heart soared at his admission. Could this be real? Clearly, 'twas a dream.

Josiah realized his presence may be intrusive — he didn't want to spy on his friend's private moment with his love. Working his way through the stalls back to the market, Josiah left them alone with their loving declarations.

"Do ye love me, Colin?"

"Can ye nay see it? I race to see you nearly every day. Ye consume my thoughts. My heart fairly beats out o' my chest when I merely think of ye. I canna focus on anything else other than ye. Your dark hair, pale skin, ample bosom—" The pink apples reappeared on her cheeks. "I want ye. I want all of ye, all the time. I want ye to be my wife. Aye, I love ye, lassie."

His words made her mind swim and her blood pulse hotly under her skin. Unlike Colin's verbosity, her words left her. She could think of nothing more than to return to his embrace and kiss him fully and completely.

"Do ye love me, lassie?" he asked into her lips. She nodded her head as their mouths remained joined.

"Aye," she breathed into his mouth, and both his chest and his cock swelled at her answer. "I love ye, ye hot-headed man."

Colin pulled the kerchief from her hair, spilling the ebony river of her locks over her back, thrusting his fingers into the lush beauty, and pressed his lips to hers again, caressing her mouth more than kissing it.

His was a heady kiss, a passionate kiss, and one that would seal their union until the priest could make it official later that spring.

The End

Love this novelette? Then keep reading for a peek at the first novel in the series: *To Dance in the Glen!* Or check out the other books by Michelle Deerwester-Dalrymple after the except.

An Excerpt from To Dance in the Glen

Northern Highlands 1296

"FIND HER! FIND HER now!"

Colin MacLeod's men immediately scattered, obeying their Laird.

The thrum of the horses' hooves on the ground made the earth vibrate in announcement. The horsemen rode hard all about the land, searching for the woman who had been missing for nearly a day.

The woman's husband, Laird of the clan MacLeod, Colin MacLeod, was beyond distraught, bordering on insanity in his search for his wife, the Lady Caitir MacLeod of MacLeod.

A tall, strong, beautiful woman with hair blacker than the night sky and the most piercing blue eyes a soul had ever seen, it was rumored that God himself crafted her body in addition to her soul, carving her out of the most coveted jewels found on earth—sapphires, diamonds, onyx.

She was truly a renowned Highland beauty.

And Colin's worried panic was spreading like a plague.

More than her appearance, however, was her very nature. While she practiced Catholicism as all good Christians did, she was raised with a deep-rooted belief in the old religion. She used herbals and prayer to heal the sick, advice and prayer to help the souls of clansmen and women who came to the Laird for help.

Caitir was genuine and honest and would give her very last shift to a poorer soul if they needed it.

What if she helped the wrong person? Colin lamented as he galloped east of the keep, his rage growing along with his dread.

It was oft said that she kept Colin grounded since Colin, though he was a full-grown man reaching nigh two score of years, could still be a rash and hot-headed man much of the time. However, just a movement or gesture from Caitir was usually enough to calm the storm that was her husband.

All these reasons and more made her the most loved person in clan MacLeod.

No one, however, loved her more than Colin. He was infatuated with her and did everything in his power to spend most of his waking moments in her presence. He scheduled hunts, farming, even his business for accounts on Market Day around Caitir and how often he could be with her. Friends and family joked about how Caitir led Colin around by his nose, or other body parts, but instead of growing angry, Colin laughed at the comments.

He knew them to be true.

But today, it was not laughter that Colin felt, it was anger and concern, more concern than he had ever felt in his life. Even more than when his oldest son had fallen off a tree and landed awkwardly. They feared that the future Laird would be crippled from a broken leg, but it turned out to be naught more than a twisted ankle, and the lad had healed fine.

This time, however, there was little hope that all would be fine.

It seemed like hours, and they still had not found her.

"Search all the way to the cliffs at the coast! Leave no stone unturned, no croft undisturbed!"

The MacLeod's voice carried across the glen.

The English had pushed farther and farther north at the insistence of King Edward Longshanks, and the sufferings of the Scottish people had increased thousand-fold. Men were slaughtered, women raped and maimed, children beaten, attacked, orphaned, or even killed. The recent events had sickened Colin, and while the English had not come as far north as Lochnora, they had come close. Now he feared that they had come too close after all.

Had I been too complacent? Had I risked too much in my pride of my clan and the security of the Highlands?

Caitir had left that morning to find marigolds, which she claimed were good for headaches and keeping bugs off other plants. While Colin was not inclined to disagree with her either way, he worried for her health. She was over six months full with their fourth child, a late baby since Ewan, their eldest, was nigh on 15 years old.

When she had not returned for a midday meal, Sarah from the kitchen had asked Keith (since called "old Keith" after the birth of his son, "young Keith," much to "old Keith's" chagrin) if he would bring a lunch to the Lady Caitir as Sarah had not seen her leave with any food, and what woman full with a babe could go more than a few hours without any food?

Old Keith rode off quickly and headed south, expecting to see the lady of the manor walking back towards the keep.

Soon though, he realized something was amiss when he reached the edge of the land of clan Lee and still had not seen Caitir, either on the muddy dirt road or anywhere in the grasses and trees close by. Without pause, Keith reined his horse around and galloped at breakneck speed back to Lochnora, screaming for Colin until his voice was ragged.

Colin was already overwrought at Caitir's disappearance, storming the keep like a tempest. He knew deep in his heart that something was not right and assembled several men to ride into the woods south of Lochnora to search for his wife when Old Keith rode up in a panic.

"My Laird. I have ridden all the way south to Lee land. 'Tis no sign of Caitir, only riders traveling the roads, and they have no' seen her," Old Keith explained.

Now Colin paled in fear, presuming the worst, afraid that the English had come farther north than ever before. Afraid that his beloved wife had encountered them.

Colin had split the search parties into two groups, one to head directly south with himself, and the other to ride with Old Keith toward the southeast in case Caitir walked far from the road. Colin thought this unlikely, but he was not a man to make assumptions. He wanted the whole of the area searched, and they would not ride home until she was found.

They split off south of the road that led north to Lochnora and south into the land of Edmund Lee and his clan. At one of the more recent market days, the Lees had told Colin of sighting the English just south of their holdings, and that was too far north in Colin's consideration. He had heard of the atrocities of the English, and had a wife, sons, and a clan to care for. Any sighting of English skin was too much.

All of this tormented Colin's mind when he heard shouting coming from the eastern woods.

Old Keith commanded his group to spread out within hearing distance to better cover as much land as possible. When he heard one of the younger men in his group (*was it Simon?*) emit a loud screech, Old Keith rode to the man's aid, only to discover the most gruesome sight a man should witness.

They had found Caitir MacLeod, wife of Colin MacLeod of MacLeod, mother of three sons, and beloved of the clan MacLeod, and Old Keith's first thought was how to hide the dear lady before Colin approached.

The English had found her.

Caitir slumped at the base of a tree, her shiny black hair now matted with dirt and blood. Her golden dress had been ripped from her, and her chemise torn up the middle, exposing her pale flesh. Her breasts were stark in the clouded afternoon sun, and there was no doubt in Keith's mind that she had been raped. However, the obviously violent rape was not the reason for her death. That was a result of the giant gash in her abdomen where her babe had lain warm and protected until this day.

So much blood.

Old Keith had no doubt as to the fate of the unborn child, and he heard Simon gasp, "Oh GOD!" then turn and sick up his morning meal into the bushes near his horse. Old Keith dismounted and walked over to the young man when his eye caught upon more blood under some brush only a few steps away.

Peering closer, Old Keith then saw the second most gruesome sight of his life. Not only had the English killed the mother, the gash in her stomach was more than a death blow—it was to remove the unborn child from the belly of the mother. Old Keith felt his gorge rise as well, with the full horror of the scene falling on his head.

She had been alive when they cut the babe from her. *Oh, God save us. God save her.* Old Keith quickly unwrapped his plaid from his shoulders and covered the bloody, dead babe in the bush.

I canna let Colin see this, he thought. *'Twill kill him as sure as I stand here.* He then turned to the others who were immobile with horror.

"Quickly!" Keith yelled to them. "Take your plaid and cover the body! Quickly, before Colin comes and sees!"

He'd barely completed his command when hoofbeats resounded in the woods behind him. He turned and saw Colin approach with his small band. Colin pulled his horse up to a halt, then dismounted, silent the whole time.

Keith moved toward him, but Colin put up a hand to stop. He moved toward his wife slowly, as if trying to understand why she lay there on the cold, hard ground.

Then he knelt to her, and placing one arm under her head and the other on her slashed belly, Colin pulled her body to his chest and cried out—a loud thundering cry of all the pain and anguish and horror that one man could contain. Then he lowered his head into that once shiny hair and cried like a child.

The men surrounding him did not know what to do. They waited patiently for the Laird of their clan to slow his tears. They watched as Colin removed his plaid from his shoulders and covered his wife as best he could with one hand, then placed that hand under her legs and lifted her to his horse.

Silently he rode back to Lochnora, slowly, his proud head lowered in defeat.

When they reached the manor at Lochnora, Colin placed her body on the table amid the keening and wailing of the women in the house. He kissed her blue lips then stood back, watching her as Alyce began to wash the body. Alyce's small daughter, Jenny, stepped forward with a thistle brush and began to work on Caitir's hair.

Soon after, Old Keith entered, a small bundle in his arms. He placed the bundle on Caitir's body, then stood back in the shadows to gauge Colin's reaction. The Laird's face twitched, and his eyes flashed with anger and pain, but he didn't move or make a sound otherwise.

Father MacBain rushed in and spoke to Old Keith first, who recommended a quick funeral, burying mother and child together. When Father MacBain approached Colin to confirm, Colin made no acknowledgment of hearing the priest's words. Father MacBain left Colin's side to begin preparations for the funeral, which was to take place the next day.

The Laird watched the preparation of his dead wife and child, staying with them the entire night. He did not leave their side, even when the clansmen took the body to the cemetery. Colin followed his wife's body through the misty rain. He watched silently as both his wife and the babe were laid in one coffin, then lowered into the ground.

As Father MacBain spoke, Colin reached down, grasped a handful of the grainy black dirt, and threw it into the grave. He stood and looked up to the sky, the light rain wetting his hair, beard, and face. Then he turned and marched back to Broch Lochnora.

He went to his chambers that he had shared with his wife, closed the chamber door, and secured it against any intruders. He stayed in that chamber, undisturbed, for six days. Not Keith, Alyce, nor his own sons could entice him to leave that chamber.

When he emerged six days later, the robust Colin MacLeod was a sickly old man. He commanded his things to be removed to a separate chamber, and he never entered his old chamber again.

Laird Colin MacLeod was a changed man from that day on.

Ten years later - 1306

Colin MacLeod watched the sunrise through the window of his chamber. He had not left the room in many days, so many days that he had lost count. It was the first time he had watched the sunrise in months, for to do so caused him a deep and aching pain, a pain that he had carried for nearly ten years. He used to take her to the grove, and they would lie near a break in the trees and watch the sun come up over the water. At daybreak, the sunlight hit the gentle waves, throwing light and color all over the grove. Caitir was bathed in a golden sheen that made her dark hair shine and her blue eyes like fire. He would love her slowly, basking the glow of the rising sun. It was how they conceived their eldest son, Ewan—a near replica of his mother, with midnight black hair and eyes that looked of dark waters.

He looked back at the chamber that had not been touched since the day she was killed. He went to her little table that held her brush and hair combs. She used to weave ribbon into the comb and wear it to the evening meal, knowing he couldn't keep his eyes off her when she had the colors of daybreak woven into her hair. Long dead flowers she had picked the day before her death rested on the table, flowers she was to dry and hang in what would be her daughter's nursery. *A daughter this time, my love,* he could hear her whisper in his ear as he took her, hot and breathless. *Aye, a daughter, with raven black hair and deep blue eyes like her mother,* he whispered back, full and panting.

They were good together. There was so much love between them—and abundance of love that they shared with each other and their offspring. Too good and too much love, Colin thought spitefully. Too much that God decided to take both his wife and their baby girl in one fell swoop. *Is it possible to have too much love?* He thought bitterly. *For God so loved the world that he sent his own son to death. Were Caitir and our daughter worth any more?* Colin thought for a moment. Though a religious man, he did accept that his wife still practiced some of the old ways, and that endeared her to him even more. Since her death, however, he questioned his faith and belief in God every day. Were his wife and their blessed daughter worth more? *Aye. God save me, but aye, they were. They did no' deserve death in return for love.* And it was in moments like this that he believed he actually hated God.

Perchance, if the death had been an accident, or quick and painless, he could have accepted their fate and moved on, his faith in God secure. But to die slowly, raped and tortured, having to watch the fruit of their love torn from her, knowing she died thusly was too much for him to bear, having borne it for nearly ten years.

Ten years. Ten years without her laugh, her raven hair that looked almost blue-black at times, her eyes that blazed with fire when she was passionate or angered. Ten years of living, knowing that he was not there for her, that he did not protect her, that *he failed her.*

His time was drawing to a close. He knew this now. He knew it the moment he saw his son lead the clansmen yesterday to patrol land and check on the croft farms. He had raised his eldest son as Caitir had wanted, strong and loyal, responsible, and somewhat moral. And if he dallied with the maids? Well, he was still young and would be married soon enough. Colin would let him have his fun.

He sighed heavily, looking towards the window again. The sun had risen, now a bright and shining ball in the spring sky. He grew sicker and weaker with each day and did not care. He did not want to be cured, forced to live longer. Having watched his son yesterday, Colin knew it was almost time and welcomed death.

A breeze stirred, and he felt a brush of air on his cheek - as light and soft as the touch of a lover's ghost.

"Soon, my love," he whispered to the empty chamber. "Soon."

Continue this exciting Medieval Highlander series that rivals
Outlander!
Book 1 - *To Dance in the Glen*

An excerpt from the Celtic Highland Maidens series

The Maiden of the Woods

Series Novella Releasing 09/28/2022!

Mid-Autumn, 209 AD, Caledonii Highlands, Alba (Scotland)

WATER RUSHED OVER KIERA'S hands as she wrung out another breacan before hanging it on the line. The weather was yet fair for mid-fall, warm enough, and the sun peeked its bright face between the clouds and burned off the morning mists. Her mother had determined it was a fine enough day for laundering and assigned the task to Kiera.

At first, Kiera had grumbled under her breath as she stirred the plaids in the cauldron over the smoky stone fire pit outside. Then her best friend, the perky blonde Bryn, joined her, easing the burden of laundry. It was enough drudgery to do it alone. Having someone help was welcome. Having someone like Bryn was a blessing from the Great Goddess.

"Och, Kiera! How does your brother get his breacan so filthy? Does he roll in the dirt with the goats?"

Kiera slung the dripping garment over the line of woven rope that hung between her roundhouse and a post in the ground. The earth beneath her bare feet grew muddy and flicked mud droplets on her ankles as she worked.

"I dinna ken. He's a man. Keeping clean is no' high on his list of concerns."

The sound of chattering voices carried across the grass, and Kiera MacBridei lifted her face toward the chieftain's wheelhouse. Two of his daughters, Gwyneth and Maeve, carried baskets on their hips as they walked toward the barn. Tall, red-headed, and powerful like their father, they were the envy of most girls in the village, and among the Caledonii tribe of the Highlands. The chieftain of Kilsyth, Ru Blogh, was renowned as one of the largest and powerful Caledonii chieftains, and his daughters followed in his mighty footsteps. Their renown among the Caledonii tribe was as great as their father's.

"Ye can say hello," Bryn said, nudging her. "Ye dinna need to hide nervously in the shadows all the time. 'Tis far more to ye than a meek lass."

Kiera dropped her eyes to the wet plaids in her arms.

"Nay, I can no' do that. I dinna know them, and what might we have to talk about? What would I say? And my father would have my hide on a stretcher if I stepped beyond his purview. He'd never permit me to become friendly with the daughters of the chieftain. He probably believes that I'd say or do the wrong thing and embarrass him. Nay, better to keep my distance." Kiera flicked her eyes to Bryn. "I'm fortunate he lets me befriend ye."

Bryn snorted. "'Tis because our mothers are close kin." Bryn moved to the other side of the line, tugging on the plaid that Kiera tossed over.

"I dinna understand why he's so angry all the time. Does your father ever break a smile?"

"No' since a Roman sword slashed his leg. His injury and limp have made him less of a warrior, so he makes up for it by ensuring no one comes close to us to begin with. He mistrusts everyone."

"He hates everyone, more like it," Bryn mumbled under her breath.

Kiera shrugged and grabbed the next plaid. She did not disagree. Her father hated everyone, even his own daughter, it seemed. Sometimes she wished she had a relationship with her father as the Chieftain's daughter had with their father, Ru.

The final batch of boiled plaid was ready for the line.

"I'll retrieve another basket," Kiera told Bryn. "Mother has extras near the lean-to."

The short stack of baskets sat askance against the daubed side of her roundhouse. Selecting a large enough basket, she hiked it to her hip as she had seen the chieftain's daughters do, and came around the side of the house.

Only she wasn't looking where she was going and crashed into a solid form of a man. She stumbled backward and was caught around the waist by a pair of strong arms.

"Och, my apologies!" Kiera burst out, thinking she'd run into her brother, Owen. Then raised her eyes. And froze.

The man in front of her was one of her brother's few friends, and a man her father hated more than any other in the village.

Cormac Innes stood near her brother, Owen, his cold green eyes staring down at her. Taller than her brother, with rich brown hair and a lean-muscled figure, he was as striking a man to look at as he was dour. As much as her father hated Cormac, it seemed Cormac despised their family right back. Owen was the only one from their roundhouse that escaped his ire — in fact, they had lately become fast friends — much to her father's chagrin.

"My apologies," Kiera said again in a much lower voice. She shifted to step backward, but Cormac didn't release her right away. His hand lingered on her lower back.

"Och, Kiera," her brother Owen exclaimed. "Ye must quit looking at the ground. Lift your head when ye walk, lass! 'Tis the only way to see the world!"

Kiera's cheeks burned as she nodded and untangled herself from Cormac's grasp. From beneath her lowered eyelids, she peeked at Cormac, who glared at her. Hugging the basket tighter to her hip like a shield, she trudged off toward Bryn.

Her friend stood stock still, her mouth hanging open.

"Kiera! What did he say to ye? Ye were practically hugging the man!"

Bryn knew of Kiera's recent girlish crush on the tall Caledonii warrior. While she had hid it from everyone until her eighteenth year, Bryn had caught her admiring Cormac from afar. She had not let up in teasing Kiera and encouraging her to approach Cormac since.

"Nay, I was running into the man. He just caught me before I fell. 'Tis all." Kiera's voice was tight, subdued.

Bryn nudged her side. "That is who ye need to say *good day* to. He will never see ye if ye hide in the shadows."

Kiera shook her head. "Nay. I dinna understand why, but Cormac does naught but glare at me. To him, I'm naught more than an irritation he must suffer for his friend."

Bryn flicked her gaze from Kiera to Cormac and back. One eye squinted as she studied her friend. "Why does he no' care for ye? Have ye asked him or your brother? If ye knew, then mayhap ye could broach him . . ."

"Bryn, nay!" She slammed the basket onto the ground. "I could no' be with someone who despises me so. And if word got back to my father, I'd suffer his wrath! Nay better to stay far away from him."

"But, if ye leave the shadows, ye might speak with him, move beyond . . ."

Kiera was done talking about hiding in the shadows. "Are ye going to help me finish the laundry or no'?"

Bryn eyed her hard, then followed Kiera to the boiling pot. She chattered away as Kiera considered what her friend had said.

Aye. He might not see her in the shadows, but Kiera was not brave enough to leave them.

Read *The Maiden of the Woods* today!

An excerpt from the
Historical Fevered series

The Highlander's Scarred Heart

Chapter One

Sean

Southern Highlands, 1335

When Sean walked into the village, he kept his head down, but he noticed the stares from under the edge of his hood, nonetheless. He tried to tug the worn leather down more, trying to hide his vicious scars that plagued his face, but a worn hood can only hide so much.

Drizzling rain helped him keep his cover — no one questioned a man wearing a hood in the rain. Yet, he still had to glance to the side, look over his wide shoulders to make sure he kept his distance, and with every movement of his hood, parts of his face peeked out.

And villagers were the worst. Nosy. Gossipy. Wary of strangers. None of which helped him as he ambled past sodden stalls and rain-soaked thatched coverings. His deep-set hazel eyes, more wary than any villager's eye could ever be, scanned the well-trod path before him.

Of course, he was more wary than any villager — no Highlander still living in the safety of their clan lands would ever know the horrors he'd seen. Sean MacDubh's caution was, if nothing else, well earned.

At the end of the pathway was the space he'd been searching for. A hooded plea to the local laird had elicited sympathy from the burly man and his dear wife. Ahh, wives . . . They were the one shining light for Sean. Their hearts were large and ready to aid those in need — the poor, the downtrodden — and they oft convinced their husbands to act with more goodwill than they might otherwise. And in this case, the comely, walnut haired lady used her womanly graces to encourage her husband to extend a small stall in the village to this artisan. Better than tithing for a beggar, she had pointed out. Disgruntled, the laird had agreed.

And here he was, walking in the rain to the stall at the end of the path, hoping that someone in this miserable village might have a need for brass buckles or a variety of beads, both of which were small enough for Sean to carry as he traversed all of Scotland, a lone journeyman with no prospects, no family, no hope for the future.

Try the Historical Fevered Series today!

If you love this book, be sure to leave a review! Reviews are life blood for authors, and I appreciate every review I receive!
Want to find me? Click her for all my socials, and where to leave reviews:
https://linktr.ee/mddalrympleauthor

1

---

1. https://linktr.ee/mddalrympleauthor

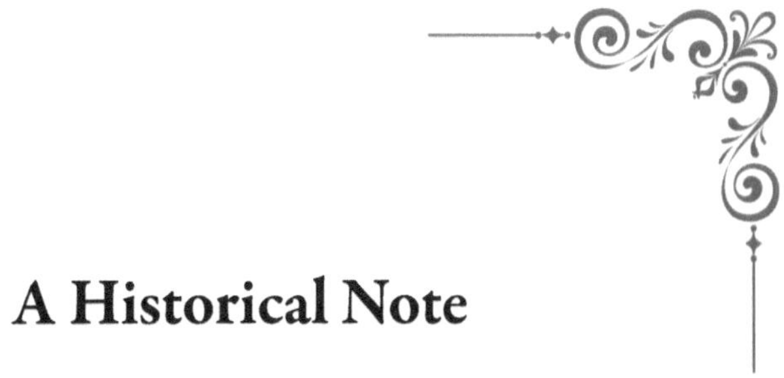

A Historical Note

As mentioned in previous books, I do try to remain loyal to the history, but I also bend historical elements for many reasons: to create a stronger setting, to make the story more vivid. Of course, for those who are familiar with the Highland kilts, you may be well aware that the traditional idea of a kilt as we love on our Highland men today became more standard, both in color for clans and in how they were worn, in the latter 1500s to early 1600s. However, they did have wool cloth, often woven into patterns, and we love our Highlanders in kilts, so I do make a suggestion of it in my books. Creative licensing! As for any other historical inaccuracies, those are mine and used to make the story as rich as possible.

A thank you to my readers

—

I would like to extend a heartfelt thank you to all of you for taking a chance and reading my first romance novel. Even with some extensive writing experience – even teaching others how to write! – actually completing a novel and publishing it involves the writer opening herself up, exposing herself in way that is challenging. That you, dear reader, took the chance to read this romantic tale makes the risk worth it.

I would also like to thank my kids and family in general for always supporting me. They always assumed writing was my real job. To my encouraging children, Mommy has always been an author. And my mom, who saw her daughter get a degree in English, of all things, and made no judgements, and instead remained confident that her daughter would be successful even with such an inauspicious field of study.

Finally, I would like to thank Michael, the man in my life who has been so supportive of my career shift to focus more on writing, and who makes a great sounding board for ideas.

About the Author

Michelle Deerwester-Dalrymple is a professor of writing and an author. She started reading when she was 3 years old, writing when she was 4, and published her first poem at age 16. With over 40 books written, she has also scribed articles and essays on a variety of topics, including several texts on writing for middle and high school students. She is also working on a novel inspired by actual events. She lives in California with her family of seven.

You can visit her blog page, sign up for her newsletter, and follow all her socials at:

https://linktr.ee/mddalrympleauthor

Also by the Author:

As Michelle Deerwester-Dalrymple
Glen Highland Romance
The Courtship of the Glen –Prequel Short Novella
To Dance in the Glen – Book 1
The Lady of the Glen – Book 2
The Exile of the Glen – Book 3
The Jewel of the Glen – Book 4
The Seduction of the Glen – Book 5
The Warrior of the Glen – Book 6
An Echo in the Glen – Book 7
The Blackguard of the Glen – Book 8
Christmas in the Glen — Book 9
The Celtic Highland Maidens
The Maiden of the Storm
The Maiden of the Woods
The Maiden of the Grove
The Maiden of the Celts
The Maiden of the Stones
The Roman of the North
The Maiden of the Loch
The Fairy Tale *Before* Series
Before the Glass Slipper
Before the Magic Mirror
Before the Cursed Beast

Before the Mermaid's Tale

------ ❧ ------

Glen Coe Highlanders Romance
Highland Burn – Book 1
Highland Breath — Book 2
Highland Beauty — Book 3
Historical Fevered Series – short and steamy romance
The Highlander's Scarred Heart
The Highlander's Legacy
The Highlander's Return
Her Knight's Second Chance
The Highlander's Vow
Her Outlaw Highlander
Outlaw Highlander Found
Outlaw Highlander Home
Her Knight's Christmas Gift
As M. D. Dalrymple:
Men in Uniform Series
Night Shift – Book 1
Day Shift – Book 2
Overtime – Book 3
Holiday Pay – Book 4
School Resource Officer—Book 5
Undercover – Book 6
Holdover – Book 7
Men in Uniform: Marines
Her Desirable Defender – book 1
Her Irresistible Guardian – Book 2
Campus Heat Series
Charming – Book 1
Tempting – Book 2

Infatuated – Book 3
Craving – Book 4
Alluring – Book 5

www.ingramcontent.com/pod-product-compliance
Lightning Source LLC
Chambersburg PA
CBHW060448160726
47992CB00003B/1128